Margaret K. McElderry Books
An imprint of Simon & Schuster Children's Publishing Division
1230 Avenue of the Americas
New York, New York 10020

First published 1989 by Walker Books Ltd. London
Manufactured in China

40 39 38 37 36 35 34

0319 WAL

Library of Congress Cataloging-in-Publication Data
Rosen, Michael, date
    We're going on a bear hunt / retold by Michael Rosen; illustrated by
Helen Oxenbury
        p.   cm.
    Summary: Brave bear hunters go through grass, a river, mud, and
other obstacles before the inevitable encounter with the bear forces
a headlong retreat.
    [1. Bears—Fiction.   2. Hunting—Fiction.]   I. Oxenbury, Helen. ill.
II. title.
PZ7.R71867We   1989   [E]—dc19   88-13338   CIP   AC
ISBN-13: 978-0-689-50476-1 (ISBN-10: 0-689-50476-4)

We're Going on a Bear Hunt

Retold by
Michael Rosen

Illustrated by
Helen Oxenbury

Margaret K. McElderry Books

We're going on a bear hunt.

We're going to catch a big one.

What a beautiful day!

We're not scared.

Oh-oh! Grass!

Long, wavy grass.

We can't go over it.

We can't go under it.

Oh, no!

We've got to go through it!

Swishy swashy!
Swishy swashy!
Swishy swashy!

We're going on a bear hunt.

We're going to catch a big one.

What a beautiful day!

We're not scared.

Oh-oh! A river!

A deep, cold river.

We can't go over it.

We can't go under it.

Oh, no!

We've got to go through it!

Splash splosh!
Splash splosh!
Splash splosh!

We're going on a bear hunt.

We're going to catch a big one.

What a beautiful day!

We're not scared.

Oh-oh! Mud!

Thick, oozy mud.

We can't go over it.

We can't go under it.

Oh, no!

We've got to go through it!

Squelch squerch!
Squelch squerch!
Squelch squerch!

We're going on a bear hunt.

We're going to catch a big one.

What a beautiful day!

We're not scared.

Oh-oh! A forest!

A big, dark forest.

We can't go over it.

We can't go under it.

Oh, no!

We've got to go through it!

Stumble trip!
Stumble trip!
Stumble trip!

We're going on a bear hunt.

We're going to catch a big one.

What a beautiful day!

We're not scared.

Oh-oh! A snowstorm!

A swirling, whirling snowstorm.

We can't go over it.

We can't go under it.

Oh, no!

We've got to go through it!

Hoooo woooo!
Hoooo woooo!
Hoooo woooo!

We're going on a bear hunt.

We're going to catch a big one.

What a beautiful day!

We're not scared.

Oh-oh! A cave!
A narrow, gloomy cave.
We can't go over it.
We can't go under it.

Oh, no!
We've got to go through it!

Tiptoe!

Tiptoe!

Tiptoe!

WHAT'S THAT?

One shiny wet nose!

Two big furry ears!

Two big goggly eyes!

IT'S A BEAR!!!!

Quick! Back through the cave! Tiptoe! Tiptoe! Tiptoe!

Back through the snowstorm! Hoooo wooooo! Hoooo wooooo!

Back through the forest! Stumble trip! Stumble trip! Stumble trip!

Back through the mud! Squelch squerch! Squelch squerch!

Back through the river! Splash splosh! Splash splosh! Splash splosh!

Back through the grass! Swishy swashy! Swishy swashy!

Get to our front door.

Open the door.

Up the stairs.

Oh, no!

We forgot to shut the door.

Back downstairs.

Shut the door.

Back upstairs.

Into the bedroom.

Into bed.

Under the covers.

We're not going on

a bear hunt again.